Bold

"Her Liberation"

By Toya J

Praise for Bold

"A riveting story woven through exotic poetry. The lust for pure freedom from anything that removes power to determine action without restraint".
— **Joyce McMillan**, Activist, Community Organizer.

"This book took me on a journey that went beyond sex, sexual desires or sexual fantasies. I was taken to another dimension, void of ego, expectations, limitations of the conditioned mind. I truly felt the freedom, ownership and responsibility the author embraced on her journey. Her willingness to be submissive and dominated was balanced with her awareness of self in commanding what it is that she truly desires. Women's liberation is an understatement. The truth contained within the author's words will serve as a catalyst for awakening. Thank you for sharing with me; I am truly honored and humbled".
— **Anthony Heath,** Health & Wellness Coach

"This collection of poetry is not only about lust, but it is also   about sexual deliverance and fantasy. The underlying message is about the freedom to grow. These poems take you on an exploratory journey. So, I hope you have someone that is ready to receive the energy you get from Toya's words".
— **Cito Blanko,** Philanthropist, Poet

Bold: *Her Liberation* is truly an example of what it means to be a liberated woman. Toya's depiction of female sexuality and desire is empowering in a world that maintains the paradox of the Madonna and Vixen. She does not water down or ask permission, which is so often required of women, but rather, displays female sexuality in a raw, honest and unapologetic way. BOLD explores the inner working of a woman addressing self-love and self-exploration that can inspire other women to reconnect with themselves in their own individual way.

– **KH,** LMHC

Toya J
Bold Her Liberation

Raised in the popular Island of Jamaica. Toya is currently a resident of New York City. She has three siblings, Is a dog lover and enjoys the outdoors. She is a kaleidoscope of inner and outer beauty with an infectious smile. She is a valuable jewel that creates an impression on anyone she interacts with and a sucker for romance. Toya is an avid reader with a vivid imagination. Whenever she is not writing or at work she can be found volunteering at midnight runs, being a co-facilitator with the Focus Forward Project at the Federal Jail or feeding the homeless on special holidays. Her hobbies are running outdoors, thinking about her next meal, trying to perfect her selfies or taking naps. Toya values her spiritual faith, family, friendship, loyalty and most importantly, her relationship with self.

BOLD is her first published book. If you wish to know when her next book will be available follow her on Instagram, Twitter and Facebook @beboldtoya to get updates regarding her next publication "Humbled".

Bold

Copyright © 2019 by Toya J

Publisher
Bold Flamingo

First Edition
ISBN- 978-1-7331814-0-2 - E-book
ISBN- 978-1-7331814-1-9 - Paperback

Printed in the United States of America

For further information or to contact Toya J
please send an email to: marie@boldflamingo.net
Toya's books are available at special discounts when
purchased in bulk for promotions or events.

DISCLAIMER OF WARRANTY

Dedication

Special dedication to the memory of my beloved Pomeranian Prince who transitioned on October 14, 2018.

I lost a part of me when you looked at me in distress, and I was helpless. Your warmth and puppy kisses will forever be etched in my heart. I will continue to carry your memories securely in my bosom. Sleep in peace, my furry friend; mommy misses you dearly.

This book is also dedicated to the women and men who suppress their feelings because of fear of being judged or who feel shackled to their cultural norms and practices. Know that it is okay to seek mental health services; don't become a victim of mental health stigma. Let it go; you are not your past. It is important for us to confront our demons so that we can begin to heal. Be unapologetic about owning your truth so that you can begin to walk in your purpose.

Prologue

Toya is my alter-ego. I quickly lost my equilibrium when tragedy vomited emotional and physical pain into my otherwise stable life. Depressed, aroused, scorched with heat for physical and emotional intimacy, my "Bold" appeared as an indescribable creature with whom I shared no familiarity. Initially I misunderstood her, but she was persistent and convenient in a supernatural manner exposing me, luring me out of my comfort zone. Toya made me touch myself repeatedly and taught me not to feel embarrassed about masturbation. Very soon, it became evident that I needed to explore my body and to enjoy the pleasures that I finally discovered.

My responses to my sexual thoughts shocked me, it appeared raw, vulgar and contaminated. Initially, I was scared and thought I changed, but no, I evolved into a free woman. I was now having a greater appreciation for the purity of sex; I finally understood what it truly meant to please myself sexually. The lens through which I now look at sex is artistic and wholesome.

Toya allowed me to embrace my woman-ness, now I can explore my body without feeling ashamed and fearful. I am preparing myself for that orgasmic experience at the opportune moment. Ironically, the free woman in me revealed herself at one of the lowest points in my life, when I was sinking deep into the abyss of depression. I had no use for her, but she coerced me to confront my fears in an organic manner in addition to seeking professional help.

Being free gave me courage, forced me to explore and ultimately to discover self. I finally connected with my feminine powers. This free woman challenged me and allowed me to have those difficult conversations with myself. This free woman made me accept my sexual individuality, comforted me when I felt alone and in despair. This free woman became me, and I became this free woman admiring the beauty of the mind and inner lust.

I resorted to writing sensual poetry to neutralize my spells of sexual desire and depression. Stimulated by erotic poetry, I explored my body and allowed my imagination to take me on a sensual journey. I allowed nature to take control; I trusted the process.

The universe aligned when I stumbled upon Voice Out Jam Sessions on August 2, 2018, a platform which allowed me to express myself and accepted my raunchy poetry. The audience embraced me. I fed their insatiable appetite with my rousing voice, sexiness and raw content. I was unapologetic and confident in my delivery. I connected with my inner lust, gained traction with the free woman. I could not deny my fascination for my new-found love: Poetry. I was sassy, raw with my renditions and highly anticipated, imaginative thoughts. I found my truth on my lustful journey, released my inhibitions, gained self-acceptance respectfully, and found my voice.

I am free.

"Caress her mind with knowledge
Stimulate her thoughts with purpose
Feed her fear with protection
Erase her doubts with consistency"
— Toya

Wintery Mix

2. Nightmare
3. Forecast
4. Sad Girl
5. Hunger
6. Scarred
7. Restless
8. Overcast
9. Alone
10. I Cried
11. Haunted
12. Darkness
13. Buried
14. Natural High
15. Scent of Orchids
16. Triangle
17. Ticking Time Bomb
18. How I Coped
19. Bondage
20. Siren

When Lust Meets Fantasy

24. Tease
25. Bitter Seduction
26. Twisted
27. That Moment
28. 7 inches

Confrontation with Reality

Acceptance

4

Wintry Mix

It was the beginning of spring, summer came. Winter prolonged for me; it was harsh, and old man winter seemed angry at me. I struggled to center myself. Rapidly I sank into a quicksand of darkness. I could no longer maintain homeostasis. I sought clarity; instead, I found grimness. I grieved the sudden loss of my independence. I was angry and questioned God I knew in my heart He answered; I just did not get the answer I sought selfishly. I was unable to see beyond my pain. My vision was overshadowed by my anger. I kept reflecting on the fact that I was in the right place at the wrong time. My blood boiled. I was innocent, just following through with my job description. I watched my life crumble around me; hope disappeared, and sadness encased me. The butterfly in me cocooned. With my broken wings and clipped beak, I was silenced and held captive in my pain. I was trapped in a physical and emotional snow storm.

I

Nightmare

I laid in bed motionless
Wishing it was the break of day
Paralyzed with fear
Pain pierced my neck
And left shoulder
The pain was intense
The heat that radiated from the restricting collar
Was
Almost suffocating
Sleep was impossible
I stayed awake for hours
Enduring my prolonged nightmare
Six weeks felt like an eternity to be confined in a restricting
Collar
I was a prisoner trapped in my own body
Recovery seemed like a distant memory when my
Nightmare was in fact my reality

Forecast

Looming   clouds   loitered
Winter   lingered
Over-exposed
Naked   and   trapped
Depression   clawed
At my fragile   psychological state
And   crippled me

Sad Girl

In the silence of the night
I struggled to hold back sobs
Somehow the tsunami of tears
Waterlogged me
Initially I was scared
I did not understand
Flabbergasted by emotions
I felt like a guest in my own body
My feelings had no respect for me
It was trifling
My feelings were so petty
They only approached me when I was alone
I was bummed
My feelings expanded
And
Led me to a familiar yet unknown path

Hunger

Lights out
    Frantically, I attempted to ignore my feelings
I knew my body craved
        A boost of intimacy
But I was at a disadvantage
           I was single
Unavailable physically and emotionally
      So, the hunger game prolonged

My
Need for romance
Dwelled
Within
                    Me
                            Like a living beast
                                    My
                            Psychological space
                                    Infected
                    Visible scars left behind
                                    With
                    A
Diagnosis
Treatment plan included
Physical Intimacy
Prescription
Not filled because
I cannot afford the co-pay

Scarred

The burden of lust

Weighed

Heavily on my chest

Lust

Yelled at me

I screamed

Restless

Over Cast

Deprived of intimacy

     Tainted thoughts cloaked me

My new reality

    My trauma

      My austere journey

    Overshadowed

       By fantasy

Unapologetic about my truth

   Within the depth of my throbbing heart

    I caved

And found shelter

Alone

Nature heard
My cry
From the pit of yearning
And
Left me stranded
This was my battle to fight
I had to figure it out
Insulated with lonesomeness
I yearned to escape

Tackled

Excruciating pain
Attacked me
While the
Urge for
Intimacy
Eclipsed me
Tear stained face saturated my pillow
Crisscrossed with
The demand for intimacy
Feelings compressed
The stationary dark horizon of pain
And need for sex magnified.
I sobbed myself to siesta

I searched for tranquility

                                   Amidst chaos

               And

Found nostalgia

       Air-whipped with deception

     I sought comfort in my reckless thoughts

Confronted with freedom I panicked

Haunted

Darkness

I suffered in the midst of the night
When mom turned the lights
Off
Tormented by
Ache
Solitude confronted the art of
seduction
And generated a
Hostile
Sleep environment
Now
Provoked and flustered
Sleep
Became a distant memory

Buried

The quicksand of lust sucked me in
I gasped for air
Energy extracted
I was
Tossed into the cesspool of time
Time was all I had

Natural High

Pain morphed
Into sexual desire
I cried out in aroused agony
Sexual hunger intensified
Petrified
I tried to suppress my natural cravings
For
Sex
Betrayed by my carnal instincts
Seduced by pain
It became
My natural high
My aphrodisiac
My love drug
Pain and need for sex unexpectedly interconnected
Filled me with anxiety

Scent of Orchids

The
        Fragrance
        Of
                Orchids
        Seduced
        Me
Blissfully

Triangle

Desperation
made me wish   I could disconnect
my brain signals   Linked to the triangle contained
within my inner thigh   Nature's treasure a pressure
Temperature elevated   Triangle   did not define me
But   Navigating these angles   And   razor-sharp urges
Surrounding the altar of my Venus.   Left me Ill at ease

On
the
verge
of
explosion
I
waited
patiently
filled
with
uncertainty
and mixed emotions

Ticking Time Bomb

How I Coped

Pain broke me
W i t h d r a w n
overwhelmed with emotions
I entertained the thought of
ending it all
Soon I realized that I was not weak mentally
It just appeared that way
Turbulence real
I had to get through the cloudy days
Survival was my only option
I had to escape the commotion
because my locomotion was no longer in
motion
I had to trim this pain
I needed to make it disappear
I had to escape
The feelings, the nightmares and the sexual desires
Solitude ravished me
No one will ever understand unless
They travelled my path
Writing saved me
Writing scared me
Writing ushered me to my fantasy land

Bondage

I collapsed to the ground
Had a concussion
Several months later
Depression enslaved me
Mental illness = BDSM
For Clarity
My depression held me in Bondage
Disciplined enough to show up for my pain management
appointments
I interacted with a Dominant called depression
I became Submissive to my physical and emotional
limitations
Sadism the assumed pleasure that my aggressor gained
from making me suffer
Mentally and physically perplexed me
Masochism the sexual gratification that transmuted
from the consistent pain I felt in my
neck and shoulders
My delicate intestines were often shoved around after my
wild imaginary sex
Limb by limb this imaginary person dismembered my body
parts
With his explosive touch
It was fantasy sex
I was
Held hostage by my uncouth imaginative thoughts

Siren

Blessed with 8000 nerve endings on my clit
Marinated sensitive nerve endings
Formed
A spicy, juicy flavour
Sunday morning
Dreary daybreak
Sun wriggled to rise
But the fire between my legs was about to cause an explosion
Luckily
The Fire Department was in close proximity
I felt an aura
Not an epileptic aura
No need to summon "Stunna Jav" to rush me to Lawrence Hospital
As
Muscle spasms raced up my dew flaps
Body shivered
Dinner roll trapped
Betwixt my legs
Secured padlock
To contain the fire that
Tenaciously throbbed amidst my thighs
Nature ran its course
Blessed indeed
I felt cursed on Sunday morning
No Kemar Highcon in sight to feed me banana
Hold-up
I have never eaten his banana for
breakfast
Snack
Or late-night treat
Still
I endorsed the Highcon
He said he was lucky but I would like to say
Blessed
Even though I have never felt or enjoyed his length

20

When Lust Meets Fantasy

I sought refuge in my writing, as I struggled to find a balance with my new normal, pain and lustful desires. I was overwhelmed with emotions, as well as the fear of being judged or looked at differently. I safely unmuted my silence in my writing because I did not want to suffer in silence anymore. Culturally I was raised not to talk about "sex" that was classified information. Implicitly I agreed and accepted this approach until recently when I started my transition into womanhood. In this context I am referring to my psychological growth. I no longer wanted to diminish who I was as an individual because of the fear of not being accepted. I unlocked the door that might not be congruent to some but during the process I was empowered, and silence was no longer an option.

Tease

Emotions ran express when he got close
So close our skins rear-ended
Mind and body conversed
Alarmingly I recoiled at the thought of falling
Too late
I was already drowning in his masculine presence
Unstable juice box spilt droplets within my inner thighs
The shocking truth of my eroticism
Numbed my delayed reaction
Banana basket screamed at me angrily
I ignored her
She twitched
Startled by this behavior I became faint and feverish
I collapsed in my bed of shameless desire

Buried under a mountain of desire
Mangled mind and flesh came to a halt
Edged on desolation
Shadows of pain and covetousness prowled
Loud silence smirked at me in an unforgiving
manner
Inundated with displeasure
Misfortune hibernated within the hollows
Of my tunnel of love
Pressure mounted in my genitalia
I tried to gather fragmented thoughts
Instead I was
Frozen with anxiety
I collapsed into the gorge of sunset

Bitter Seduction

Twisted

Salacious thoughts haunted me as I sped
Across the bridge swiftly in my trench coat and stilettos.
Pleased with my nakedness
Armed with enthusiasm to see my clandestine lover
Succulently I licked my lips

I
Glanced in the rearview mirror and envisioned the burning
Passion
In his eyes
Screeching tires jolted me back to reality
I swerved from the approaching car
The moisture between my legs accelerated my drive
I pulled up
There he was
Standing

Our eyes locked and kissed each other
I dropped my coat
Lover enticed
He devoured my body with his eyes
He smiled a cracked smile and launched at me steadily

My body released
I screamed, opened my lids and welcomed him
I whimpered in a gentle manner
When he made his grand entry

He

shifted gears

I bounced with him

In his monologue, he begged me to loosen my grip,

Instead, I clutched him possessively

He yelped in agony

I felt the added lubrication as he expanded in me

I pushed harder against him and constricted his
Extension
He squealed with beats

Our

Sweaty
Slippery
Bodies made music
We
Soared to the apex of desire

7 Inches

I

                  Welcomed

The

                    Thought

Of

        Him

Making

                      Love

       To Me

In

                      My

Red

       S
       T
       I
       L
       E
       T
       T
       O
       S

Paradise

I experienced that unadulterated sex
Raw sex
We explored
The depth of each other's nakedness
It was exciting

And

Wholesome
My calm cuddle hormones amplified
I relaxed
Flooded eyes sparkled with enchantment
His thunderbird sauntered into my phoenix nest
Desire liquefied
Formed puddles

My fancy article greeted his love muscle
I sobbed
As he crafted love notes all over my insides
Fast and furious strokes
Flesh to flesh
Legs wrapped around his bare buttocks
Nails buried at the nape of his neck
He
Pierced me with slow accurate blows
Clutch tightened
Warm juices freed
With definitive tenderness

Asylum

My

        anigaV walls

Created

        A sanctuary for

His

        sineP

Intensity

I

Was
So

D
E
E
P

In
His
Salacious thoughts

I

Ejaculated

He feasted on my crimson velvet body
I indulged in his sensuous delight
He loved the fact that I had those
baby-making hips and hedonistic eyes
I seduced him with the overly suggestive
Gait of my hips
He stripped my scantily clothed body
Anxiously laid me on my back
Kissed me ravenously
Explored areas of my body
My body shivered with delight
As
He massaged me playfully with the warmth
Of his breath
I moaned with satisfaction
He stroked his skin flute with excitement
Awakened further immeasurable erotic
Thirst
He fired his piston
Into
My moisture filled honey pot
Articulated
Delightful cries replaced my agonizing
Supplication
With quickened pace his depth maximized
I
Discharged profusely

Juices seeped through my furry furnace
Lubricated cockpit gripped his jackhammer
I shrieked with gladness

                                                    My

Love making sounds sent him in an erotic frenzy

                                                    I

Welcomed his mania
Ferociously he pushed
Against my cervix
My rose buds opened and absorbed his cucumber
He released in my passion pit
Bodies
Contracted

                                                    And

Milky white fluids escaped
Formed an alliance with his sperm

Breathless

It is not about the climax
Take me to the next pinnacle
Stimulate me; make me moist
I will do whatever you want
                              If
            You promise to make me forget how to breathe
            It is not about the anticipated volcanic eruption
                              I have screamed enough
        I just never knew how it felt to forget how to breathe
                              This is the moment I craved
                              Let us make it memorable

Slowly kiss me
Position yourself
Let me straddle you
I want to feel all of you
Make me forget how to breathe

                                        Hold me
                                        Touch me
                                        Feel me
                As my muscles contract around your shaft
Focus
Let me ride your surfboard
Pull me closer
Go deep
Deeper
Make me forget how to breathe

Addicted

He
My ocean
Logics blurred
Wholeheartedly, I dived in
Magnetic force
Dominated my innocence
Energies crashed
Fearlessly
I surrendered
Floated into his harbor
His emerald eyes pierced my soul
Unmasking my silent trepidation
I
His muse
His hidden obsession
Right crevices navigated
Tongue slid into my narrow passage
He licked my cherry
Sweet to taste
He was addicted
I
Experienced explosive orgasm
Lovely sentiment
I was
Addicted

Penetration

I squealed out in idyllic agony
As his ruler recklessly measured the yardage of my water
well
My natural juices
Gushed over his face
He smiled leisurely as he inhaled my after-sex fragrance
Like angelic doves, we tossed and turned light heartedly
Curled toes
Arched limbs
He separated my cringed legs
With masculine force
Self-sacrificing for instant gratification
I conceded
Smiled
Fingers penetrated me blissfully
Bodies moved in alliance
We
Glided
And
Beamed sinfully at each other

Rendezvous

Perspiration dripped from my body forming rivulets on
The sheets
My body he caressed with tender, soft touches,
Fingers and tongue worked simultaneously
Body sculpted into various positions for accurate pleasure
The magic he created with his tongue shocked my body
I experienced fast and hyperbolic climax
I lost gravity
He grabbed my legs
Secured them firmly to the bed post
My
Weak body twisted
Hands tied
Escape barred
Targeted
Sex slave for the night
Screams blocked
He smiled roguishly
Extended man umbrella inspected my honey pot
He pounded me mercilessly
I travelled to ecstasy
He owned my body
And
Demanded my attention with every stroke
Limp body responded eagerly to his request
I emulated the rhythm of his body
Climax clashed like the ocean hitting
The rocks with excessive force
Left us entangled with each other

Swift strokes
I caught onto his pace
My
Honeysuckle sweetened his custard launcher
I summoned him to my pleasure spot
Induced strokes
Stirred my pelvis
I
braced him with my thighs
Indicating that he needed to change his stride
He responded because of our strong connection
coupled with
The fact that he aimed to please
Lowered pace
Improved sexual traction
And magnified our climax

Home Run

My insatiable appetite
For
Good sex was admirable
Yes
Good sex
Good sex equivalent
To a full course meal
Appetizer - foreplay
Side Order - excessive clitoral stimulation with a tongue
Feather, vibrator or finger
Main Dish - penetration
Dessert - communication topped with hot chocolate
Free woman
Requires good sex
Mind blowing sex
That involves an experienced lover
Giving me that
Euphoric feeling
Leaving my slippery slot
        D   r   i   P
Dripping like a popsicle

Desire

Sultry sounds of his voice
Provoked and sweet-talked me
While
His
Words
Fondled me
Funneled
Sensual shivers down my spine
And
Massaged my prickly pear

Attraction

Watching me with such intensity
Slower your thoughts
Get undressed
As I
Slip seductively out of my silk dress
Slowly exposing perfect breast, I looked at him
Teasingly
My dress fell to the floor
He stood spellbound
Our gaze locked
He licked his lips
Kissed me zealously
Traced my lips with the tip of his index finger
Our encounter was tantalizing
He pulled me to the bathroom and ran a bath
With extra bubbles
Lowered me gradually
Without losing physical contact
He wanted to get closer, and closer
He moaned anxiously
I silenced his moan with lethargic kisses
He threw caution out the window
And
Connected me to seventh heaven

Beneath the Sheets

The white crisp sheet enveloped my russet frame
Curvaceous   contours   outlined
Seemingly innocent and pure
Captivated   my   lover's   eyes
Nerves fluttered
As he
Contemplated his approach.
Smitten   by my   perceived innocence
Healthy bloom in my cheeks evoked
Strong sexual desire beneath his
waistline
I knew how to get him aroused
Enchantingly I caressed my lips
Sensuously   I   moved   my   body
He   stood   transfixed
Our eyes   searched   each other
Fascinated   by his   seductress
His   clarinet   whistled
At   my   golden   arches

Scream

I whimpered in pain
Ouch
That was the ultimate sign for him
To check in with me
But
He was too focused on his nut
I yelped
His stroke deepened
The elasticity of my vagina
Stretched
Adjusting to his shaft
I needed him
To control
His strokes
Instead
He pounced
In and out
Rapidly and selfishly

Climax

He gripped my wrist with such force
Sunk further into my crack
Free hand clutched my passion pit
As
His master sword descended deep into my
Pandora box
The ride got rigid
Pressure built up
Ride slowed
Enraged
With
Every thrust of his hips
I choked with passion
Gave into his sexual demands
Matched his energy
He screamed in agony
And
Climaxed

Nakedness

I want to experience that kind of nakedness
Beyond the physical
To be naked with his thoughts and feelings
When I attempt to undress him
I want to peel away the layers of
His psychological scars
I want to meet him at the intersection of his
Thoughts
The crossroads of his emotions
The dead-end of the state of his
Unconsciousness
As we approach those difficult conversations
That we swore we would never have

I want us to feel safe with each other
Emotionally
Now that is my idea of nakedness
Because I am capable of undressing him
Physically
With my eyes and salacious thoughts!
His thoughts and feelings are restricted

45

Lust

Exploring
   Hidden crevice of each other's landscape
   Hypnotized by the harmony of his touch
   Hungrily he watched
     As I played with my catfish
     He
     Initiated the next move
       And
       Held a steadfast gaze in silence
       As our undecorated flesh spoke to each other

Liberated

I
Scanned the structure of his face
With passionate kisses
Moist tongue
Explored the contours of his lanky body
He
Shivered
Restlessly
I roamed the rough exterior of his frame
Hungrily like a savage
I
Sunk my teeth in his bare flesh
He
Cringed with pain
Yet
Shrieked with pleasure
I
Caressed his lips
Tongue
Plunged into his warm mouth
Overlapped each other
With sexual hunger
We explored each other

Slow Cooking Sunday

Sweet aroma escaped the kitchen
Lazily, I shifted in his bed
I felt a sharp prick on my leg
To my surprise he left me several roses
Where he recently slept
Nipple ring tugged at the sheet and pierced me

I

Arched from the sharp pain
Concealed my nakedness
Picked up the love note that he left
Trailed
The rose petals to the kitchen

He

Dragged the sheet from my body
Gripped my ass
Tossed me on the kitchen counter
Fondled my breast
In his baritone voice

He

Ordered me to lay on my stomach
I arched my body as his tongue licked me playfully
I was
In heat and not in the mood to be slow cooked
I was fully marinated
And
Did not mind that he would have me rare

Sunrise

I saw my reflection
In him
He mirrored my existence
Electrifying expression
Amped up my libido

I
Conformed to his rhythm
Controlled thrust
Heavy breathing
As
His sun rose
In my chamber

Morphine

Sex with him   felt like anesthesia
as the feelings   exited my body
and
numbed
me

Universe

I rotated around my galaxy of feelings
To escape my planet of discomfort
Thoughts would saunter to fantasy
Ecosphere
Crammed
W
I
T
H
Lovemaking
C
U
D
D
L
I
N
G
And heavy petting

Novelty

M   Y

Chocolate frame melted on his
Chiseled torso
Sticky mess formed
He licked me in a painstaking manner
Thickened molten chocolate devilishly good
I became crisp on the edges
He treated himself to my confectionary
Drenched he swirled in my sugar encrusted   S
                                                     K
                                                     E
                                                     L
                                                     E
                                                     T
                                                     O
                                                     N

His love was the perfect blend
Of soothing aromatherapy that hugged
The
Gaps of my
Heart
Mind
Body
And soul
Nourishing me with comfort

Lavender

Storm

Crumpled linen sheets with his musty cologne
Replaced
My once methodical space
His cracked smile provoked me
As
He followed the trail into my forest
I was free
Alluring with an infectious smile
He caught my spell
But that did not interrupt
His lust
He was enchanted by my perfectly soft lips
And favoured my
Curved hips

56

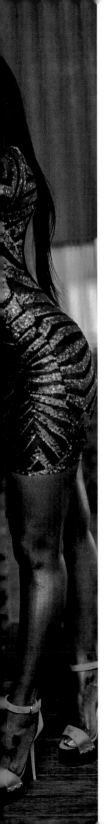

Confrontation with Reality

    I led myself to believe that he was a good fit. I could not contain my excitement because he presented well. I thought I hit the "lottery". In retrospect, I'm not sure why I led myself to believe I lucked out because I did not play the lottery. In my desperation to feel wanted, I became distracted with the figment of my imagination as opposed to the reality of the situation. I saw all the warning signs, but I ignored them because of my need to belong.

Caged Pussycat

Veins and arteries
  Chilled with emotions
I yearned to be touched
  By a courageous lover
One with an
Open mind
I no longer
Wish to be a risk- averse lover

Mask

Mystery box unlocked
Leaving volcanic vibrations
Friction brewed
Explosive thoughts erupted
Naked truth of my carnal desires
Exposed
The depth of my deep sea
Left open

Naive

His
perceived
openness
to
experience
with
me
excited
me
I
shared
his
enthusiasm

Awakened

He stimulated me intellectually
While
I sat on the bar stool salivating
Tequila affectionately slithered down my throat
I twitched with anxiety
My body came alive
I pondered
Was it the warmth from the tequila
Or
Was it the intimate space we shared
I looked
At his perfectly manicured fingers
Imagined them
Fondling my fish mitten
Ok
Stop it
I
Inhaled
Exhaled
Contained intense pulsation
Crossed and uncrossed legs
Humidity accumulated rapidly
No
No
Such a gentleman in the moment
Nipple erection concealed discreetly
Eyes connected

My inner sex
Throbbed fervently
Gently he held my face
Kissed me hungrily
I
Caught on
To the rhythm of his tongue
Responded accordingly
Honestly
I wanted all of him
Secretly
I imagined roaming hands
Discovering my curves
I wanted him to punctuate my sentences with
Kisses
And
Ejaculate in my soul

Kiss That

Fused our saliva

And

Locked our lips

Betrayal

Heart stood still
    Feelings derailed
    Pressure built up in my chest
    Restricted air passage
    Gasped for air
    Palms sweaty
    I
Lost control
Startled
Color faded rapidly from my body
Paled
Lips
    Flushed cheeks
    He slighted me
    Showed no remorse
    He was
    Heartless
    Stoic

Seductress

I seduced him with my infectious smile
I knew I wanted him the moment
Our eyes smooched
If only he knew the hairs on my kitty throbbed
With delight
I contained my emotions
I wondered about the length and width of his shaft
Curiosity got the best of me
I lured him onto the dance floor
I was so close to him I saw my reflection in his
Sweat
He was in a daze
He was clueless that this was foreplay
That
I desired to explore
I sought to experience an orgasm with him
He was my fantasy
I was disheartened
That I never felt his erection
I separated myself from his embrace

Dance

He instructed the beats of my heart
I tuned out internal dialogue
Feelings flowed
I danced with the state of my being
Expressed my feelings
He made a good impression
I kept dancing
I swirled with my feelings
Enjoyed his beats, increased tempo
Released safety breaks
Emotions led me
I danced
Enjoyed his dominance
Vivacious hips thrusting against hips
I hated the "Tango Dance"
It was the dance of sorrow
Overwhelmed with joy
I danced with my date
Fluidity of our bodies twirled
Perfection
Sure, this dance would prolong
Steadily I fell for the rhythm
He braked unexpectedly
I moved my hips back and forth to re-engage him
Languid movements turned icy

Chilled me
I smiled
Embraced him heartily
Flirtatious gestures met
His
Repulsive attitude
No spark of passion left to ignite
Alarmed by his abrupt arctic demeanour
I blamed it on the music and alcohol
I was in denial
About his bipolar ass
Yet, his polar gaze froze me
I was frantic
Dejected by his insecurities
I stood on the dance floor
Asphyxlated by the icy air that stood between us

Feelings

I allowed myself to feel
I got rid of my rules
I believed him
I felt the somersaults in my gut
He never felt
He never got rid of his game
He never believed in me
He never felt those butterflies
He just wanted to have sex
I understood the game
I was still deceived by my innocence
He created the illusion of possibilities
But it was mere lust
I caught on before it was too late

Crushed

I was
Trapped in the valley of yearning
Mood draped outward
Hanging onto the branches of desire
Tangled
And stretched thin
No longer in control
Roots sprung inward

Acceptance

I was able to separate my intentions from the way others may experience me. Now, I am at peace with myself. My unconventional ways may not fit within the confines of what I should be, but most importantly, I am able to live with my decision. I confronted my fears, and freedom enveloped me. I have come to the realization that if I live my life to please others, I am at a disadvantage. Unfortunately, everyone is entitled to their opinion. I accepted self with all of my flaws, fell in love with me and moved forward to the next phase of my journey!

Saved

God heard my

Cries
From

The pit of yearning
And
Rescued
Me

Rebirth

Enough tears shed
Endless nights spent
Listening
To the deafening echoes of my heartbeat
Silently I suffered
No more
Puddles of tears left in me
The melody of my heart beat pumped
Energy
I am alive
BRISKLY
I walked away
Never to   look back

Closure

Perverted hunger fed me hope
Gave me a holistic cleanse
Through narrative therapy
I felt
I imagined
I penned my thoughts
I fantasied
I inked my feelings
I self-reflected
I communicated with my inner me
I am a new creation
A better version of self
I am free

No Regrets

The incessant pain took me on a **J** o u r n e y
that I tried to **I** g n o r e
It forced me to feel and experience **E** m o t i o n s
that I thought were **D** o r m a n t
I can't say
I have **R** e g r e t s meeting lust
Because
T o d a y
I stand
L i b e r a t e d

Me First

I will continue   to wait patiently
I refuse to   place a timeline
On my future orgasmic experience
And
I refuse   to settle
I have the   power to decide
I control   my narrative and
I acknowledge
The power   I possess
Internally & Externally

Artwork

I DECORATED
My CANVAS
With my raw EMOTIONS
Intentional brush STROKES
Created
My graphic MASTERPIECE
I re-captured   my voice through my art
No longer   will I be silenced

BOLD / Toya J

"Seek to find self this is the greatest form of discovery" – Toya

"Support is felt not heard" – Toya

Heartfelt Acknowledgement

John F. Kennedy once said, "As we express our gratitude, we must never forget that the highest appreciation is not to utter words but to live by them". Without his grace and mercy, my creativity would be stifled. I have to thank GOD for giving me the strength, perseverance, insight and patience to carry on when I was overwhelmed and floating in doubt. Most importantly, it is a privilege and honour to have a bond and attachment with my parents and sisters. The love I have for you all is indescribable. I appreciate you all individually and collectively. To my Brother- Jhavagne Dunn (@stunnazentertainment) you have impacted my life in such a profound way. Without your unconditional love and concrete support my trajectory would look a lot different. Thanks for being such an amazing gentleman in my life and know that I love you completely. Many thanks to Bertha Patterson, Gaitrie Hulasie, Cecil Palm, Dayshana Monroe, Tracy Crockett, Crystal Cox, Alissia Lopez, Stephanie Asante, Juliet Wright, Nigel Baker, Everett David, Nichole Robinson, Paulette Palmer, Tarik Q. Shah @Quotethemc.

To Moe Suso thank you for illuminating the true essence of friendship. Whenever I called you, all you ever said was "Toya, I got you". You shared your home by allowing me to capture special moments for my photoshoots and entertained my crew members. Most importantly, you were consistent and very resourceful.

To creatives:

Photographers-@Piktureperfect, @meschidaphilip, Make-up artist- @luvlyneeks18, @ spbeauty_, Body Paint Artist- @Kervyn5, Tattoo Artist- Shellsink, Cover Designer-

Creativeankh.com, Editor @soulmuze, Interior Book Layout @ victorkwegyir, Musical Artist@ thecelebritty_, Author/ Editor/Book Coach @Mellmotivates, Mentor @ceoazarel, Social Media Manager @iamester. I thank you all for bringing my vision to life.

To the reviewers Joyce McMillan @jmacforfamilies, Anthony Heath @ lean_buddah, Cito Blanko @Citoblanko, Licensed Mental Health Clinician-KH, I am forever filled with gratitude that you took the time out of your busy schedules to read my manuscript

Thanks to my Angels, Andrea Green for her creativity with my vibrant, flamboyant hairstyles and Denise Wright for your moral and concrete support. You both embody the idea that "support should be supportive". I love you all, Angels.

To Voice Out Jam Sessions, thanks for your acceptance, as well as the platform created for other creatives to express ourselves without feeling judged every Thursday night. You guys and gals are my extended family.

Coordinator/Host- Damion Hawthrone
Producer- Andre Hawthorne
Email-Dretegsmusic@gmail.com
942 East 233rd street
Bronx, NY
646-705-3409

It is impossible to list the names of everyone who had an input; even if I did not list your name, I appreciate you all. To my future readers, thanks for your purchase!

Made in United States
North Haven, CT
15 September 2023